W9-DFH-279

Kidnapped

Robert Louis Stevenson

Academic Industries, Inc.
West Haven, Connecticut 06516

ISBN 0-88301-717-2

Published by
Academic Industries, Inc.
The Academic Building
Saw Mill Road
West Haven, Connecticut 06516

Printed in the United States of America

ABOUT THE AUTHOR

Robert Louis Stevenson, a British essayist, novelist, and poet was born in Edinburgh in 1850. From infancy he battled with poor health, nearly dying in 1858 of gastric fever.

Stevenson attended schools in Edinburgh from 1858 to 1867. After his health improved he followed the family profession of civil engineering. Even though he greatly enjoyed the outdoor life of an engineer, it was a strain on his physical endurance. From engineering he turned to law and finally to writing.

In the summer of 1886 he published *Kidnapped*. No one order of popularity can be established for Stevenson's books. Whatever placement his books are given, however, Stevenson will long be remembered as a man who contributed some of the most stimulating writing in English literature.

Robert Louis Stevenson
Kidnapped

Alan Breck

Ebenezer Balfour

Mr. Rankeillor

David Balfour

Captain Hoseason

With all my strength I pulled away and ran to the rail. The boat was moving away toward the town, my uncle in the stern. He turned and showed me his cruel face. . . .

Help!
Help!
Help!

COVE

It was the last I saw. Already strong hands had pulled me back from the rail, and now lightning seemed to hit me. . . .

And I saw a great flash of fire and fell to the ground. . . .

That does it, men. Put him below!

It all began with my father's death. That morning in June, in the year 1751, I left his house at the age of seventeen.

I'll be sorry to leave Essendean, but I must. . . .

I was met by the village minister, Mr. Campbell. . . .

Hold on, Davie lad. I'd like a word with you.

I've been meaning to say goodbye, sir. . . .

Before your father died, he gave me a certain letter, which he said was yours when he died, Davie. . .and to start you off to the house of Shaws, where he came from and where he said you might return. . . .

The house of Shaws? What had he to do with that?

Why the name of that family, Davie boy, is the name you bear, lad. . . Balfour of Shaws. An old and honest house, although perhaps now run down. . . .

It says To the Hands of Ebenezer Balfour, Esquire of Shaws, and will be delivered by my son, David Balfour. . . .It sounds too good for a poor lad like me. Should I go?

To the hands of EBENEZER BALFOUR, Esquire of Shaws and will be delivered by my son DAVID BALFOUR

Yes, lad. Cramond is about two days walk, near Edinburgh. I would hope that they would welcome you. But remember Mr. Balfour is the master of the house and treat him with respect.

Well, sir, I'll try.

By the second day I was in Cramond. . . .

Can you tell me where the Shaw house is?

What! Lad, stay clear of that house!

And after two or three had given me the same look and answer, I began to think. . . .

It be none of my business, laddie, but stay away.

There must be something strange about the Shaws.

And the next man I asked told me plainly. . . .

Tell me, sir, what kind of man is Mr. Balfour of the Shaws?

What, boy? No kind of man at all!

It was at sundown when a woman stopped.

That is the house of Shaws! Blood built it; blood stopped the building of it; blood shall bring it down!

W-what?

If you see the master tell him Jennet Clouston has put a curse on him and his house.

But I carried my father's letter and would not be stopped. . . .

Well, anyway, I'll knock. . . .

My knock ignored, I pounded the door angrily until. . . .

This is loaded! What do you want?

I come with a letter to Mr. Ebenezer Balfour of Shaws. Is he here? It is a letter of introduction!

A what? Who are you?

They call me David Balfour!

Upon hearing my name, the old man was quiet and then. . . .

Is your father dead?

Much surprised at this I found no voice and stood staring. . . .

Yes, he'll be dead, no doubt; and that will be what brings you here.

Then there came a great rattling of chains and locks, and as the door slowly opened. . . .

Go into the kitchen and touch nothing!

The burned up fire showed me the poorest room I ever put eyes on.

Nothing on the table but a bowl of oatmeal, a spoon, and a small cup of beer. . .not another thing in this great empty room.

Let me see the letter then.

The letter is for Mr. Balfour, and no one else.

And who do you think I am? Your father was my brother. Little as you may like me, David, I'm your uncle, and you're my nephew. So give me the letter and sit down to some oatmeal.

He's not one I would choose for an uncle.

And as my uncle, bending over the fire, turned the letter over in his hands. . . .

Do you know what's in it?

You can see for yourself the seal has not been broken.

No, but you'll have had some hopes, no doubt?

I did hope I had rich relatives here to help me in my life. But I have some money.

I look for no favors from you and want none that are not freely given.

Hoot-toot! Don't get huffy with me, Davie. We'll agree fine yet. If you had enough to eat, come away to your bed.

To my surprise, he didn't light a lamp but led me into the dark hallway, feeling his way. . . .

I cannot see, Uncle.

Hoot-toot! There's a fine moon! Lights in a house is a thing I don't agree with, Davie.

And showing me my room in darkness, he pulled the door closed, locking it from the outside. . . .

Please sir. Give me a light to go to bed with.

Good night, Davie. I'm afraid of fires.

The room was as cold as a well, and the bed, when I found it, damp and cold.

Lucky I've got me bundle and blanket . . .I'll sleep on the floor. . . .

And at the first light of day. . . .

Aye! This was a fine room at one time. Ten years ago or perhaps twenty.

Hearing my shouts, my uncle let me out and led me back to the kitchen. . . .

Have your breakfast. Davie. I'll give ye anything in reason.

He's a real miser, all right.

Then, at the end of our meal. . . .

Davie, you've come to the right place when ye came to your Uncle Ebenezer. I've a great love for the family, and I mean to do right by you. Meanwhile, no letters, no messages, no kind of word to anybody. . .or else you'll have to leave!

Uncle Ebenezer, I would have you know I have feelings. Show me the door and I'll go.

13

Later in a room next to the kitchen where he told me to go, I found a great number of books. . . .

Now what's this? Was my father the older brother?

To my Brother Ebenezer on his fifth Birthday from Alexander

Was my father older or younger than you, Uncle? Or were you twins?

What makes you ask that?

Take your hands off me!

What?

You shouldn't speak to me about your father, Davie. That's where the mistake is.

What do you mean?

He was all the brother that I ever had. I'll say no more!

Something odd here. See how he is shaking!

A story came into my mind of a poor man that was a rightful heir and a wicked brother that tried to keep him from what was his. . . .

Why did this talk about my father upset him?

So we sat watching each other without another word to say, like cat and mouse, until. . . .

David, a promise is a promise . . .and I've been thinking that I promised, before you were born, a little bit of silver. . . It was between me and your father, nothing legal, you understand. . . .

Now what is he up to?

I believe it's forty pounds exactly.

He's making up the whole story. But why?

And if you'll step outside the door a minute just to see what kind of night it is, I'll get it out for you.

Very well, Uncle.

I'll go along with him.

It was a dark night, and it looked like there was a storm coming up. . . .

I'll wait awhile, let him think he's fooling me. . . .

But when he called me in. . . .

There you are, Davie! I'm a strange man, but I'll show you I keep my promises!

Gold and silver coins! He meant what he said!

I could hardly believe it. . . .

No, I want no thanks, I do my duty. It's a pleasure for me to help my brother's son.

But I recovered to thank him as well as I could. . . .

That was very kind of you, Uncle.

You need not thank me, Davie. But will you do me a favor now?

Of course, Uncle.

Well, you know I am growing old, and this house and garden can use some help, lad. . . .

Pulling a rusty key from his pocket then. . . .

Here's the key to the tower at the far end of the house. Bring me down the chest that's at the top of the stairs. There are papers in it.

Very well.

When I asked for a light, he said no lights in his house. . . .

Very well. Are the stairs good?

They're grand. But keep to the wall, there's no railing.

Feeling along the wall in the black night, I came to the tower door. . . .

I had just turned the key when a flash of lightning lit up the whole sky. . . .

The tower was never finished.

Blinded by the sudden change from light to darkness again, I stepped into the tower.

I felt my way up in the blackness with beating heart.

He said no railing. I'll stay close to the wall.

The house of Shaws stood five stories high, and as I climbed higher. . . .

Odd! It seems to be getting lighter. . . .

17

Suddenly, there was a second flash of lightning.

I seem to be climbing on an open stairway!

My heart froze, then turned to anger.

Grand stairs, are they! He meant to kill me!

I crawled on slowly as a snail.

I'll test every inch of the way now.

It had become dark again, and suddenly there were many bats flying down from the top of the tower, beating upon my face and body.

And then, coming close to another turn, my hand slipped.

There's nothing beyond. . .nothing but emptiness!

The stair had been built no higher. Another step would have sent me straight to my death!

He is trying to kill me!

I climbed down again with anger in my heart.

As I approached my uncle's house there came a flash of lightning which showed him waiting and listening. . . .

He acts as if that thunder was the sound of my fall!

Then filled with fear, he ran into the house.

I followed him quietly into the kitchen and watched him take a bottle from the closet. Trembling, he drank from it.

Stepping forward suddenly I grabbed him from behind. . . .

Aha!

Hey. . . what. . . .

And he tumbled to the floor like a dead man. . . .

Aaahh!

Snatching the keys I went to the closet before he should get up. . . .

Hmm. . .moneybags . . .papers. . .that knife might come in handy. . .

Hiding my knife inside my coat, I turned to my uncle. . . .

He looks more dead than alive. . . .

But after I threw some water in his face. . . .

Are ye alive? O man, are ye alive?

I am, small thanks to you!

The little blue bottle . . .in the closet. . . gasp. . . .

In the closet I found the bottle of medicine with the instructions written on a paper.

Here you are. . . swallow!

Ahh. . .Davie. . . it's my heart.

Why have you lied to me? Why do you fear admitting you and my father were twins? Why did you give me money? Why try to get rid of me, even to kill me? Why, uncle?

Gasp. . .no more now . . .let me go to bed, Davie. . .I'll tell you all in the morning!

Locking him into his room, I built up the fire.

Perhaps by morning I'll know some of the mystery behind all this.

Morning changed, and I could hardly wait to take the upper hand.

I think it is time now for us to understand each other! You took me for a stupid country boy. I took you for a good man. It seems we were both wrong. . . .

No more talk now until after breakfast, Davie.

Suddenly I heard a knock at the door.

Sit where you are, Uncle. I'll see who it is.

I opened the door, and there stood a boy in sailor's clothes.

What's up, mate?

What is it? What's your business?

My name's Ransome. I've brought a letter from old Hoseason to Mr. Balfour, and I'm hungry as a whale.

Come inside then.

My uncle read the letter while I gave the lad some breakfast. . . .

Suddenly my uncle handed me the letter.

Read that!

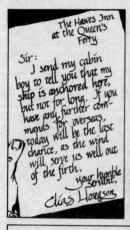

The Hawes Inn at the Queen's Ferry

Sir:

I send my cabin boy to tell you that my ship is anchored here, but not for long. If you have any further commands for overseas, today will be the last chance, as the wind will serve us well out of the firth.

your humble servant,
Elias Hoseason

Mr. Hoseason is a captain of a trading brig, called the Covenant, Davie. I do business with him, and if we could walk over with this lad, I could see the captain at the Hawes Inn or maybe on board the Covenant if there are papers for me to sign. Then we can go over to the lawyer, Mr. Rankeillor. . . .

There will be many people at the harbor. My uncle won't dare to try anything there.

He's a highly respected old man, and he knew your father.

Very well, Uncle. I'll go with you to the ferry.

I'd like a closer view of the sea and ships after living all my life inland.

Ol' Cap'n Hoseason is no seaman. It's Mr. Shuan who sails the brig. He's the finest sailor on the seas, except for when he's drunk. I've been at sea since I was nine.

It sounds great, lad. Do they treat you well?

Then Ransome opened his shirt, and showed me great scars and tatoos on his chest. . . .

I've done a lot in my life. Stealing and even murder. This is how they treat me, but you'll see, I'll get back at them.

I know a trick or two to get even. But it's not a bad life.

The boy is crazy and that ship the Covenant sounds like a bad dream upon the seas.

Coming to the top of the hill, we saw a skiff waiting to take the men. . . .

There's the skiff waiting for the captain, and out there is the Covenant getting ready to sail.

I ought to tell you, Uncle, there's nothing that will bring me on board that Covenant.

What's that? Well, we'll have to please you, Davie. We'll head for the inn.

At the inn, Ransome led us upstairs to a small room. . . .

The room's hot as an oven, and this man is bundled and buttoned to the neck. . . .

Here they be, captain.

I am proud to see you, Mr. Balfour, and glad that you are here in time. The wind's fair and we'll be sailing soon.

Captain Hoseason, you keep your room too hot.

It's my habit, Mr. Balfour. I have cold blood, sir. There's neither fur, nor cloth, nor hot rum will warm me.

Er. . .it's too hot for me. . . .

Why not run downstairs then for a while, Davie. . . .

Sickened by the hot room and wanting to take a look at the sea, I was fool enough to let my uncle out of my sight.

I'll leave them to their papers and business.

The smell of the sea made me think of long trips and faraway places.

And soon returning to the inn. . . .

Buy me a drink, Davie.

Sure, Ransome, what'll you have?

As we sat drinking, I noticed the landlord leave.

Excuse me, sir, do you know a Mr. Rankeillor?

What, yes, and a very honest man.

You're not a friend of Ebenezer Balfour?

Er. . . no, sir.

Good. He's a wicked old man. There's many would like to see him hanging from a rope. Did you ever hear that he killed a man. . . a Mr. Alexander. . . just to get the Shaws place?

Was Alexander the eldest son?

Ay. What else would he have killed him for?

So Ebenezer killed my father, the rightful heir to the house of Shaws. Then Shaws belongs to me!

Staring out the window later I saw Captain Hoseason on the deck among his men.

The men seem to like him.

And when he returned, my uncle called us together.

Lad, your uncle tells me great things about you. I wish we could be better friends but time is short. Would you come on board and have a drink with me?

I'd like to, captain, but my uncle and I have to see a lawyer.

Yes, he told me of that. But the skiff will take you ashore at the town dock, close to the Rankeillor's house.

Well. . . .

Suddenly, leaning down, he whispered in my ear.

Take care, lad. He means to do you harm. Come aboard till I can get a word with you.

I went with him toward the skiff. . . .

What luck to have found a friend and helper!

Let's go, lad.

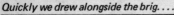
Quickly we drew alongside the brig. . . .

And almost instantly I was lifted into the air and set down on deck.

With all my strength I pulled away. . . .

Let me go!

And ran to the rail of the ship.

There was the skiff heading for the town, with my uncle in it.

Leaving me! I've been tricked!

And as I cried for help, his face turned showing me a look of cruelty and terror. . . .

Help! Murder!

But it was the last I saw as strong hands grabbed me, and lightning seemed to strike my head.

When I returned again to life, I was in darkness, in great pain. . . .

And later. . .after a long wait. . . .

Bound and dizzy, I hurt in every bone until. . . .

And soon I was carried up to the forward deck where again I lost my senses. . . .

The sailors were rough men. Some had sailed with pirates. Some had escaped from the King's ships, and they often fought among themselves.

Take that.

Oof!

They're tough and rough enough but kind to me.

Ransome, the young cabinboy, came in from the cabin nursing new wounds.

What happened to your face?

Mr. Shuan hit me. I'll get him back, you'll see.

Meanwhile the Covenant was being tossed about on heavy sea and making little progress.

Suddenly my life as a prisoner changed one night when. . . .

Here! Ransome's done for!

Why? Is he dead? But how. . .?

Dead enough. Mr. Shuan gave him one too many.

And then to my surprise Captain Hoseason spoke to me. . . .

We want you to serve in the cabin. You'll be changing places with Ransome. Get along with you!

The brig was rolling on a long cresting wave as I ran across the decks. . . .

Ohh!

Grab a rope, son!

And again only saved by the kindness of one of the hands on deck. . . .

Hold tight, laddie!

Help!

Then I learned we were sailing northeast around Scotland.

I thought we were halfway across the Atlantic!

Not in these winds. We've got to sail north first!

Later that night Captain Hoseason spoke to his chief officer. . . .

You drunkard! You've murdered the boy!

Well, he brought me a dirty cup!

COVENANT

For my new duties, I brought them food and drink, glad of the work which kept me from thinking.

The boy's death troubles me. I'll have another glass!

My story will be the boy went overboard. Who's to tell?

Ay, who's to know as don't already.

Another week and more ill luck drove the Covenant this way and that until. . . .

Ahoy! Boat to starboard. Watch the rocks!

They're waiting for their supper below. . . .

Suddenly the ship hit something. . . .

We've hit a rock!

No, sir. We've only run a boat down!

In the fog we had run down a boat and split her in the middle.

We can save that man!

Drop a line!

33

As he was brought into the cabin....

I'm sorry, sir, about the boat!

More than the boat, some good friends of mine have gone to the bottom.

I can tell by your speech that you are a Scotchman. Why do you wear a French soldier's coat?

You are thinking, perhaps, of turning me over to the British soldiers?

Don't be so fast, man. I won't give you over to the soldiers.

There's thirty gold coins for you if you put me ashore on the coast, or sixty if ye take me into port.

You must be working for the honor of Scotland. Sixty gold coins and I won't say a word.

Good!

As the captain left, leaving me with the Scottish rebel....

And so you're a revolutionary?

Ay, and you by your long face must be loyal to the King.

Although I was loyal to King George, I could understand this man working for King Louis of France, so that he could smuggle gold across for his chief who was fighting to win back freedom in Scotland against the King's men.

I can see your point. Your chief is in France, then?

Ay, and this money I carry is part of the rent King George is looking for. Will you fill this bottle for me.

Needing the key, I went back to the Captain. . . .

Captain, the bottle is empty, and the gentleman would like a drink. Will you give me the key to the locker?

Why here's our chance to get him out of the cabin!

Ay, we can both grab him before he has time to draw his sword.

As I heard these evil men planning, I was filled with fear and anger.

You see, David, that gentleman is a danger to the ship, besides being an enemy of good King George!

The guns are in the cabin, David. Ye might pick up a pistol or two to help us.

And I give you my word, David. If you help us you'll have some of his gold.

Very well, sir.

But upon returning to the cabin, I knew I could not go through with it.

Do you want to be killed? They're all murderers here. They've killed a boy already. Now it's to be you.

Ay, but they haven't got me yet.

Will you help me? What's your name?

That I will. I am no thief and no murderer.

Thinking a man with such a fine coat liked fine people. . . .

I am David Balfour of Shaws.

My name is Stewart. They call me Alan Breck.

As Alan prepared to fight. . . .

I must warn you, there are fifteen men against us!

Well, that can't be helped! I'll face the door and you keep loading the pistols.

But there's a door behind you, Alan.

Ay, you'll have to guard that door and the skylight too. If they come, you must shoot!

Suddenly the captain came to the door.

Halt!

A sword? Is this how you repay us?

The captain gave me an ugly look.

My sword has killed more enemies than you have toes on your feet! Call up your men and fight!

David, I'll remember this!

The sea was quiet, but I was unable to hear voices.

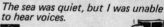

Get ready now for they are coming!

And as the attack began. . . .

That's him that killed the boy, Alan!

Never you mind. Look to your window!

As I turned to my place. . . .

And it was my turn to act when five men came up with a large beam for a battering ram to knock the door in. . . .

At my second and third shots, they broke and ran. . . .

As Mr. Shuan sank slowly lower, he was dragged from behind, away from the roundhouse. . . .

I hit one, Alan. I think the captain.

And I've gotten two. But that's not enough. They'll be back. To your watch, David!

Unless we can beat them once and for all, there'll be no sleep for us. This time will be for keeps!

As I waited, pistols ready. . . .

Here they come!

Suddenly the glass of the skylight was broken in a thousand pieces. . . .

But I could not pull the trigger until he grabbed me and. . . .

I'll get you, you little. . .ugh!

As he fell to the floor, I shot at another man coming through.

Agh!

Hearing Alan shout for help, I turned. . . .

Get him off me!

And catching up my sword before we were lost. . . .

But before I could help, they began to run. . . .

Come on and fight!

Help! Run!

He's like a crazy bull!

At every flash of his sword there came the scream of a man hurt. . . .

Ahhhh!

Ughhh!

He chased them along the deck, and when he turned back at last, they were still running and crying out as if he were still behind.

And am I not a good fighter? There's four down by my sword!

David, I love you like a brother!

And as I made up my bed on the floor, he stood guard, pistol in hand and sword on knee, three hours by the captain's clock.

You're a brave lad. You'll do well to get some sleep, Davie. I'll do the first watch.

After my watch with still nothing happening, I saw the brig had drifted near the coast. . . .

At six o'clock we made breakfast.

We'll hear more of them before long. The rum and brandy locker's here, and while you may keep a man from fighting, you'll never keep him away from his bottle.

Then, taking a knife, he cut one of the silver buttons from his coat. . . .

I got them from my father Duncan Stewart. It's a keepsake for last night's work. Wherever you go and show that button, the friends of Alan Breck will know you.

And later Mr. Riach called for a parley.

This is a bad job, Davie. The captain would like to speak to your friend. At the window, perhaps.

Can we trust him?

He gave his word, and the captain drew near.

Put that thing away! Have I not given my word?

Captain, last night you gave me your word, and you know what happened then. Why should I believe you now?

You've made an awful mess of my brig. I haven't enough men to sail her. My first officer is dead. Killed by your sword. We'll have to sail back into Glasgow for more men.

That won't do. You'll have to set me ashore as we agreed.

But none of us know this coast and it's one very dangerous for ships.

Then you're as poor a sailor as you are a fighter. Just set me ashore within thirty miles of my own country, except in the country of the Campbells.

It will cost money. Sixty gold coins if you can tell us how to get there.

Well, I'm more of a fighting man than a sailorman, but I know this coast pretty well.

One more thing. We may meet up with the King's ship. What then?

Captain, if you see the King's flag, it shall be your duty to run away.

Late that night under a rough sea. . . .

My brig is in danger. Come out and see what ye can do!

43

Suddenly the captain pointed into the water. . . .

There's the sea breaking on a reef. Do you know where we are?

These'll be what they call the Torran Rocks. They are about ten miles long.

There's a way through them, I suppose?

No doubt. But where?

Well, we're in for it now, Mr. Riach. Go take a look. We'll have to come in as close as we can.

Soon Mr. Riach called back. . . .

Sea to the south is rough. It seems calmer near the land.

Well, we'll have to try it. Pray God you are right.

As we got nearer, the reefs were close showing us our danger. . . .

Change course! Change course!

This is not the kind of death I fancy.

What, Alan? Surely you're not afraid?

Then the tide caught the brig and turned her into the wind. . . .

Keep her away! Watch the reef!

The wind's gone out of her sails!

And the next moment we hit the reefs. . . .

What happened?

We hit the rocks!

And as the brig began breaking to pieces. . . .

Lower the boat! We've hit ground!

Alan, do you know this place?

Ay, we're near the island of Mull.

The worst possible place for me. . .the land of my enemies the Campbells! It's covered with redcoats!

Suddenly a huge wave rocked the ship. . . .

Hold on, Davie!

I can't. . . .

And I was thrown over the side into the sea.

I went down, swallowing water as I went.

I would surely have drowned, but then. . . .

Then I was in quiet water. . . .

The moon shone clear when I finally struggled ashore. . . .

At daybreak, climbing a hill, I looked for the brig.

Not a sign of her. She must have lifted from the reef and sunk. The skiff is gone too.

My way to the mainland was blocked by a narrow strip of water.

I'm trapped here. I'll starve or freeze to death. . . .

After one hundred hours of cold and hunger, I remembered the tide.

What a fool I've been! The sea dropped to this level twice every twenty-four hours when the tide was out, and I didn't have the brains to think of it!

At first the house I came to. . . .

Ay, lad, there's been a boat ashore. Your shipmates, was they? Ay, I fed them the day after they ran ashore.

Was one of them dressed like a gentleman, with a feather in his hat?

There was no feather, laddie. But ye must be the lad with the silver button! I've word you're to follow your friend to his country by Torosay.

Thank Heavens! It was Alan!

Later.... Since the rebellion, these Highlanders aren't allowed to wear their regular clothes...they're like beggars!

They spoke no English and answered my questions in Gaelic, a language I did not understand at all....

Torosay... Torosay. Which way?

At last, my gold coins were a help to me....

For five gold coins, I will take you to Torosay, laddie....

Very well. But I warn you, don't try to cheat me!

But after a day of travelling, he sat down.

It'll cost you five gold coins more or I'll forget the way.

So that's it!

And suddenly he drew a knife from his rags....

Hoot, man you will notice this blade is sharp!

Yes, and so is my temper, you thief!

And forgetting everything but my anger....

Here's something for you to remember!

Agh!

Finally, at Torosay. . . .

Here's a shilling. I'm looking for Alan Breck Stewart.

Ay! You're the lad with the silver button, you will not be needing to offer your dirty money to a Highland gentleman.

Look out for the red soldiers, lad. Also there's the Red Fox to keep away from. He's a collector of all the taxes here and an enemy of Alan Breck. He's the King's man, the Red Fox! Also known as Colin Roy Campbell!

Later after crossing the water and being set ashore. . . .

This is Appin, Alan's country. It should be safe. . . .

Suddenly. . . .

That must be the man they call the Red Fox! But I've nothing to fear. I am an honest subject of King George!

And so, foolishly, I stopped them. . . .

Can you tell me the way to Aucharn?

The outlaw chief James of the Glens lives there! I am the King's man here with soldiers at my back! You're a bold one to ask!

Suddenly from higher up the hill. . . .

Oh, I am dead!

As he fell, I saw movement up the hill. . . .

The murderer! I see him!

And as he ran, I chased him. . . .

I see him. . .a big man in a black coat. . . .

When behind me. . . .

Stand! Come back or we fire!

What?

And as the soldiers began to spread and run after me, my heart came into my mouth with a new kind of terror.

Catch that lad! He's an accomplice!

They're after me!

And as I stood helpless with fear. . . .

Duck in here!

What?

Alan Breck! It's you!

Ay! Come along for your life!

He ran quickly among the birches, crawling on all fours, until. . . .

I can't go on. . . .

You have to. Come!

And I followed him until we didn't hear the sound of the soldiers. . . .

Just a little further and we can rest!

How does he do it?

Until at last Alan threw himself down, and we lay panting like dogs.

Ah! We'll rest a little bit here.

But when he rose to go on. . . .

You and I must part, Alan. I can't forget that murder behind me of the Red Fox! Why did you do it?

You mean you didn't do it? Thank God. Then it must have been that man in the black coat!

I'm not sure about his coat. I think it was blue.

Blue or black, do you swear you don't know him?

Ach, I've a grand memory for forgetting, Davie.

What? If I were going to kill a gentleman, would I do it on my own country and bring trouble to my clan?

We've not much time to argue. We must get out of this country. Myself since I'm a deserter, and you because you're wanted for murder!

But I am innocent. Why should I fear the justice of my country?

Ay, the same justice as the Red Fox found a while back!

True, but I can't run for something I never did.

We're in the Highlands, Davie. When I tell you to run, take my word and run. Unless you prefer to lie in a redcoat prison!

I began to think he was right. . . .

There's your choice! The redcoats! Either run with me or hang!

All right! I'll stay with you!

We'll head for Aucharn, the house of my cousin James of the Glens. I must get my clothes, and my gun, and money to carry us along.

Later that night. . . .

James must have lost his mind! If this were the soldiers, instead of you and me, he'd be in trouble!

But Alan whistled a secret signal and shortly. . . .

James Stewart, this here is a young gentleman of the Lowland. We'll not say his name.

I've heard about the accident, Alan. It will bring trouble on the country.

The Red Fox was killed in Appin. It's Appin that must pay, and I am afraid for my family. I'm thinking we must bury your clothes. They'll search us all!

What? Bury my French clothes? No!

I'll take those, and we'll need money and weapons, James.

And when he returned dressed in his French clothes. . . .

We've food for you and your friend, Alan. . .weapons, too. But we've hardly any money.

This won't do. I need money for my chief in France!

This is no time to worry about money, Alan. If you are blamed for this day's accident, then I am too, for I am your relative. And if I was to hang. . . .

Ay, that would be a bad day!

I'll have to offer a reward for you myself if they force me. To protect myself. You'll have to be out of the country, and out of Scotland, you and your friend!

What? And he is to be accused too?

But my plain common sense set me off. . . .

Why not set the blame where it belongs. . .on the man who fired the shot?

What is he saying?

Ay, and what would his clan think? Don't you think Davie the lad might be caught?

Ah, so you do know the murderer! Well, Alan, I am your friend. If I can be helpful to your friends, I won't fail you!

Ah, Davie, you're a good lad.

Tomorrow there'll be a fine show of troops. We had better be gone!

And so we set out again, heading eastward over the same broken country as before. . . .

Tomorrow there'll be a fine to-do in Appin with us gone!

Remember, Alan, I know nothing about this fight.

And as it became morning. . . .

Gasp. . .he doesn't get tired!

Come on, Davie. I've got to pass the news on to my friends in that house . . .we can't have them caught by surprise by the King's men!

Soon we were in a great valley far from any house. . . .

Ach! This is no place for you and me. They're bound to watch here!

With that, he ran harder than ever down to the water.

Come on, Davie. Jump, don't think!

But those falls. . . I'm. . .afraid!

But I forced myself to follow and. . . .

I've got you, lad. But there's more to go. . . .

It's hang or drown, Davie!

I. . .I can't. . . .

I flung myself across with a kind of anger. . . .

Then we were off again until. . . .

Then pulling me up with his leather belt. . . .

When I awoke. . . .

Be quiet, Davie. There's redcoats about!

There's no chance. They're all about!

But after a hot day on the rock. . . .

As well as one death as another. . . .

And again we made a run for it. . . .

And the next day . . .and the next. . . until. . . .

I can't go. . . another . . .step!

It's all right, Davie. . . I'll carry you.

Until at last. . . .

On the other side will be your lawyer to see . . .and I'll be pushing on to raise money for my chief!

Come with me, Alan. If things go well, there'll be money enough for us all.

Davie went to the lawyer's house in Queensferry while Alan waited in hiding.

Mr. Rankeillor? My name is David Balfour.

David Balfour? Come inside please and state your business. And where have you come from?

I have come from a great many strange places, sir. I have reason to believe I have some right on the estate of Shaws.

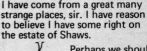

Perhaps we should go inside where we can speak privately.

And so I told Mr. Rankeillor the story of my life and recent adventures. . . .

And then my uncle had me kidnapped by Captain Hoseason and taken to sea. . . .

How awful! Go on. . . .

But when I came to tell about Alan, Mr. Rankeillor quickly stopped me. . . .

David, I am a man of the law, and if you have made friends with any outlaw, it would be better if I knew nothing about it. Already I have forgotten the name you just told me, and you may do us all the favor of not saying it again!

From this point on I called Alan "Mister Thompson," and soon finished my story.

It's an amazing story, David. And your friend Mr.-ah-Thompson sounds like a gentleman and a true friend, even though he does not obey the laws of our good King George.

I believe the estate is yours, David. But a lawsuit, in this case, would not be easy, for if any of your doings with your friend -er- Mr. Thompson were to come out, we might find we were in great trouble.

The important thing then is to make him pay for my kidnapping.

Between us we made a plan which would force my uncle to admit to the kidnapping and my rights to the estate. I then took Mr. Rankeillor to the place where Alan was hiding, and the three of us set out for the Shaws. . . .

It's a clever plan, Davie, and I'm glad to be able to help you in it.

It's in your hands now, Mr. Thompson.

When we reached the Shaws, Alan went straight to the door while Mr. Rankeillor and I hid ourselves beside the corner of the house.

Ebenezer Balfour! Come out, I'd have a word with you.

What's this? What brings you here at this time of the night?

It's about your nephew, David.

David, is it? Well, what's on your mind?

I'll be brief, sir. A ship went down near Mull, and my friends found a lad there who claims you're his uncle. They're holding him there, at great expense, and I've come to tell you you'll not see him again unless we can come to some agreement.

You'll get no ransom money from me. I don't care much for the lad myself.

Then perhaps you'll be paying us to keep him, sir. For he's got a pretty story to tell about how you had him taken out to sea by a Captain Hoseason to be murdered.

It's a lie! I gave Hoseason twenty pounds for the selling of the lad in America. There was never a word about murder!

Upon hearing my uncle's confession. . . .

Thank you very much, Mr. Thompson. . .and. . .good evening to you, Mr. Balfour.

Good evening, Ebenezer.

My uncle was in a state of shock. . . .

Come, come, Mr. Balfour, you must not be downhearted, for I promise we shall make a fair deal with you.

Mr. Rankeillor and my uncle soon came to terms, and it was agreed that Ebenezer should remain at Shaws, but that I should receive two thirds of the yearly income of the property.

Congratulations, lad!

And here is a letter to my bankers, David, placing money in your name. This will get you started in your new life.

But later as Alan and I walked away together, we thought only of our old life. . . .

Well, Davie lad, our ways are parting at last.

I shall make plans to find a safe way for you to get to France, Alan, and send you some money. . . .

We spoke very little for our hearts were sad, and I dared not look him in the face for fear of crying. . . .

Well, goodbye.

Goodbye.

COMPLETE LIST OF POCKET CLASSICS AVAILABLE

CLASSICS

C 1 Black Beauty
C 2 The Call of the Wild
C 3 Dr. Jekyll and Mr. Hyde
C 4 Dracula
C 5 Frankenstein
C 6 Huckleberry Finn
C 7 Moby Dick
C 8 The Red Badge of Courage
C 9 The Time Machine
C10 Tom Sawyer
C11 Treasure Island
C12 20,000 Leagues Under the Sea
C13 The Great Adventures of Sherlock Holmes
C14 Gulliver's Travels
C15 The Hunchback of Notre Dame
C16 The Invisible Man
C17 Journey to the Center of the Earth
C18 Kidnapped
C19 The Mysterious Island
C20 The Scarlet Letter
C21 The Story of My Life
C22 A Tale of Two Cities
C23 The Three Musketeers
C24 The War of the Worlds
C25 Around the World in Eighty Days
C26 Captains Courageous
C27 A Connecticut Yankee in King Arthur's Court
C28 The Hound of the Baskervilles
C29 The House of the Seven Gables
C30 Jane Eyre
C31 The Last of the Mohicans
C32 The Best of O. Henry
C33 The Best of Poe
C34 Two Years Before the Mast
C35 White Fang
C36 Wuthering Heights
C37 Ben Hur
C38 A Christmas Carol
C39 The Food of the Gods
C40 Ivanhoe
C41 The Man in the Iron Mask
C42 The Prince and the Pauper
C43 The Prisoner of Zenda
C44 The Return of the Native
C45 Robinson Crusoe
C46 The Scarlet Pimpernel

COMPLETE LIST OF POCKET CLASSICS AVAILABLE
(cont'd)

SHAKESPEARE